EXP ECT ✗NG

SHANNON FREEMAN

SADDLEBACK
EDUCATIONAL PUBLISHING

Lexile:

HL420

AR BL: 4/6

AR Pts:

GRAVEL ROAD

Bi-Normal

Edge of Ready

Expecting *(rural)*

Falling Out of Place

FatherSonFather

Finding Apeman *(rural)*

A Heart Like Ringo
  Starr *(verse)*

I'm Just Me

Otherwise *(verse)*

Roadside Attraction *(rural)*

Rodeo Princess *(rural)*

Screaming Quietly

Self. Destructed.

Skinhead Birdy

Sticks and Stones *(rural)*

Teeny Little Grief
  Machines *(verse)*

That Selfie Girl *(verse)*

2 Days

Unchained

Varsity 170

SADDLEBACK
EDUCATIONAL PUBLISHING
www.sdlback.com

ISBN-13: 978-1-68021-063-7
ISBN-10: 1-68021-063-7
eBook: 978-1-63078-379-2

Printed in Guangzhou, China
NOR/1015/CA21501470

20 19 18 17 16   1 2 3 4 5

Dedicated to Harbin Rose. You inspired me every step of the way.

KAELYNN

Kaelynn normally walked around barefoot. Today was different. It was an extra-hot Texas summer. She could feel the ground through her flip-flops. She was dressed for the hot weather. Polka-dot bikini top. Short cutoffs with the pockets hanging out the bottom. Her wavy brown hair hung around her face. It was freshly washed. The scent of shampoo lingered. On a day like today, it would take minutes for her hair to dry.

She was walking to Samantha's house. She knew she would have to pass a farm she loathed. The people neglected their animals. She hated passing there. You could smell the stench for blocks. The other route would take an additional ten minutes. It was too hot for that. She held her nose and tried to breathe through her mouth. As soon as she passed, she took a huge breath. She was blocks away from her destination.

As she approached, she could see there was a new pickup in the driveway. Samantha's place had a revolving door. She was thirty-one and liked to party. Hard. It took a toll on her looks. The men who came around were overweight and struggling. They always took care of Samantha, though. That was a requirement, or they wouldn't be around for long.

Kaelynn walked down the gravel driveway. She peeked inside the pickup to get some idea of what she was walking into. Country music CDs. A little rap. Some work equipment. And a city badge hanging from the rearview mirror. *Another fat bald guy. Ugh!* she thought.

She walked around back to the garage. Five people were talking. They had beers in hand and a blunt going around. Kaelynn knew everybody there. Everybody knew her except for one new face. She assumed he was the owner of the pickup. She had to admit, Samantha had come up. This wasn't one of her normal guys. He was gorgeous, with blue eyes, dirty blond hair, muscles, and a full sleeve of tattoos on one arm. His jeans sagged just enough to make him look young and fresh. Kaelynn could not keep her eyes off him.

When they were alone, she moved closer to the fan, which was the only breeze in the hot garage. Her wavy hair blew wild as the fan whirled.

"I'm Will," she heard him say from behind her.

"I'm Kaelynn," she said, turning around to look at him. She felt light-headed. She didn't know if it was the heat, the weed, the beer, or just Will's presence. He was like a dream come true. Her heart seemed to skip a beat when she looked into his blue eyes. He walked over toward the fan to steal some of the air she was enjoying. He reached over and moved a curl from her face.

Just then, the rest of the group returned. They had gone inside to get cool cups for everybody.

"What is this?" Will asked curiously.

"You've never had a cool cup before?" Kaelynn asked. "You are definitely not from around here."

"You're right," he said, tasting the frozen drink. "That's good. Really good."

She laughed. "They are. I grew up on these things. My grandmother used to sell them. All you have to do is make some Kool-Aid. But it has to be really sweet. Pour it into the cup and freeze it. Couple of hours later, cool cups."

"Cool."

Samantha seemed to notice something brewing between Kaelynn and Will. She had invited Will over, wanting to get to know him better. Kaelynn was intruding. Darn her high school body and good looks.

"Don't you have homework or something?" Samantha

asked, interrupting their conversation. "I know you didn't pass all 'dem classes this year."

"Summer school is over, Sam. Thanks for your concern."

"You're still in high school?" Will asked, shocked.

"Yeah, one year left. But I'm legal," she lied, looking over at Samantha, who rolled her eyes. She was only sixteen. She didn't want Sam to out her. Time to leave. "Hey, Will, do you mind driving me home? It's starting to get dark, and I hate to walk this late."

"Girl, walking is in your blood. I just saw your mom pass by here earlier today." Samantha knew she would hit a nerve with that. Kaelynn's mom was the neighborhood drug addict. All she did was walk around looking to score. Kaelynn lived with her grandmother. She'd lived there for as long as she could remember. Samantha knew the history. She chose this moment to use it against her.

Kaelynn looked up to Samantha. Like a big sister. But this guy was making her mean. Kaelynn shot her a look and walked toward Will's truck.

"Hey, Sam, thanks for having me over," Will said, following Kaelynn to the truck.

"Any time," Samantha said, flirting shamelessly.

Will unlocked the doors. The two climbed in.

"Hey, you mind if we go smoke a cigarette before I go home? Sam has my nerves bad," Kaelynn said.

"No, it's cool, but I don't smoke. I dip snuff."

"It's okay. I have my own smokes." She began beating the back of the cigarette pack as she explained where to find a remote location. She led him to an abandoned baseball field. It hadn't been used for years. There was talk of getting it cleaned up, but nothing had been done so far.

Kaelynn jumped out of the truck and walked toward the bleachers. Will joined her. She took a drag of her cigarette. Then exhaled as she thought about Samantha's words. "In your blood." She hated what Sam had implied. Everybody in the whole damn town thought she would turn out like her mother. Yes, she liked weed. She liked beer. Her mom was a whole different bird. She liked drugs. All kinds. The hard stuff too. She would do anything: coke, meth, crack. It didn't matter as long as she got high.

"You okay?" Will asked.

She had almost forgotten he was there. "Yeah, I'm fine," she said, smiling. She blew smoke out of her mouth. Then she leaned over and kissed him. When she was done, she lingered close to his face. "I've been wanting to do that since I saw you," she whispered.

"Me too," he said, grabbing her and pulling her close.

They kissed for what seemed like forever. Then they got back into his truck. She didn't know if it was the weed or the alcohol, but she couldn't control herself. Her brain didn't say stop. And her body responded instinctively.

He had never asked her how old she was. She hadn't asked him either. Their mutual attraction had been enough. It was as if they didn't want to know. They both figured it was better that way.

CHAPTER 2

YESSENIA

Yessenia sat on the toilet in disbelief. She stared at the pregnancy test in her hand. If she stared at it long enough, maybe it would show a different result. It was the second one she'd taken. She thought the first test was wrong. This stick had just confirmed her greatest fear. She was pregnant. *Pregnant!* The last thing she'd ever wanted to be. Everyone in her family had a ton of kids. She wanted no part of it. Now here she was.

She was on the pill. How could this have happened?

There was a loud knock on the bathroom door. She knew it was Dante.

"Yessie! What the hell? They're outside!" Dante screamed.

She rolled her eyes. At that moment she hated the sound of his voice. He turned her stomach. This was all his fault.

She told him they shouldn't have sex. That they were too young. But he said he had needs. Well, look where his "needs" had gotten her.

She wiped the tears from her face. And she washed her hands before joining him and his friends in the car. They already had two blunts going when she got there. All the windows were up. They were "hotboxing," as they liked to call it. Normally, she was down, but all that smoke was making her feel ill.

She'd mixed some tequila with Sprite before leaving the house. She took a gulp. She had to make it through this night. She was not about to do it sober. Then she took a huge drag on a blunt. She made her signature smoke rings. Her stomach began to calm down. She knew she'd been feeling a little under the weather. And so tired. But she never thought she was pregnant.

"Yo, can we roll down the windows?" she yelled, trying to talk over the music. She could feel herself getting light-headed. They had a thirty-minute drive ahead of them. She wasn't going to make it at this rate. She leaned over to Dante. "Hey, I'm not feeling so good."

"What's wrong?" he asked.

"I don't know," she lied. "Can we pull over for a second?"

Dante quickly got his boy to pull the car over. Yessenia jumped out. She began retching. Then she vomited. Dante came to her, but there was nothing he could do. Her friend Sofia was right by her side, holding her hair back.

"Dante, I have her. Are you okay, Yessie?" Sofia asked.

"It must have been something I ate. I'll be fine."

"Are you sure? We can't have you getting sick on the way back. There's too much at stake here," Dante said.

"I'll be fine. I'm always fine, right?"

They joined their friends back in the car and took off again. They smoked another blunt before pulling up at the store.

"You sure they got bank like that in here?" Dante asked Sergio.

"Man, my cousin's working the register. They got it. He told me. We just drove thirty miles. You want to chicken out now? Man—"

"Nah," Dante said. "As long as you know we're about to come up, I'm good. I'm not trying to risk everything for two dollars."

"Look, they are taking in five grand a night at this liquor store. You know they're right next to a dry county. This store is jumping."

"It don't look like it's jumping right now," Yessenia said. She was skeptical.

"That's 'cause my cousin told me when to fall through. I ain't no dummy."

"All right. Well, let's go," Dante said.

They pulled on ski masks and took out their guns. Yessenia jumped into the driver's seat. Sofia got in the passenger's seat. Yessenia turned the car toward the interstate. Sofia kept an eye on the store. Yessenia focused on the road ahead. It wasn't their first rodeo. She had been the getaway driver many times. Sofia always had her back. They were both good at it. The guys knew they could count on them. Yessenia was old-school and played her role. She was a ride-or-die type chick.

"They're coming," Sofia warned her. "And it looks like they've got company."

Yessenia clenched the steering wheel until her knuckles were white. She heard the store's alarm and knew it was time.

The guys jumped into the car. Both were yelling, "Go! Go! Go!"

She saw a man pointing a gun directly at the car's tires. She heard the gunshot. A bullet hit the dirt as she cut a hard right. She looked in the rearview mirror. The store got smaller and smaller. The guys took off their masks and put away their guns, but she was focused on getting to a safe location. Adrenaline was pumping. She felt alive. On fire.

"I hope y'all got enough money," she said, looking at them in the mirror. She didn't play about her cut, and they knew it.

LYRIC

The night of the County Connection had finally arrived. Lyric and her girls had waited for this since the last one. There were no cute boys at their school. You had to scan the whole county just to find a hot one. Lyric did a twirl in front of the mirror. She pulled down her miniskirt just enough. She didn't want to look slutty. As her best friend's car pulled into the driveway, Lyric added some lip gloss.

"Uh-huh," she said, blowing herself a kiss in the mirror. She knew she was on point.

She jumped into the front seat of the Jeep Cherokee. There was an unspoken rule between her and Stephie. Nobody rolled in front but the two of them. If Lyric was driving, Stephie knew her spot would be waiting as well.

"Oooh, girl. Look at you. Outfit on point. Makeup on fleek. I ain't mad at you."

"There you go with that dumb *fleek* stuff. Just say I'm cute, 'cause you know I am. Hey, ladies," she said to her girls in the backseat. "Let's go show these county fools who's in charge." They let out a little scream as they hit their signature dap. "Oh, let's get a pic before we roll. Give 'em something to hate on till we get there."

ؚ

They looked good. Miniskirts, fresh extensions, and only the best makeup MAC had to offer. Their walks let everyone know they had arrived. They served it just enough to not look conceited. Conceited was not cute.

Local restaurants and businesses sponsored the party. Each year the function grew bigger and better. It was the fifth annual event, and it was turned all the way up.

Lyric lingered by the refreshment table after putting in an hour on the dance floor. She was sipping her soda when she looked up and noticed a guy. He was looking directly at her. She couldn't take her eyes off him. He was a magnet, and she was caught in his magnetic field. She turned around to find Stephie.

"Girl, look at that dude over there in the baby blue."

"Which one? Not that white boy."

"You know I'm an equal opportunity chick. He is 'bout my type."

"You know I like mine tall and chocolate."

"He's chocolate, girl. It's just white chocolate."

"Well, don't turn around 'cause white chocolate is on his way."

"Yo, can I get you a drink?" he asked.

Lyric could feel his breath on her neck. She knew if she turned around, they would be too close for comfort. She took a few steps forward and turned to face Mr. White Chocolate. She shook her beverage cup. She could take care of herself.

"Well, what *can* I do for you?" His smile was killer. It was tough for Lyric to fake indifference.

"You're not from around here," she said matter-of-factly.

"Why you say that?" he asked, licking his lips in a way that made Lyric's world move in slow motion.

"Your accent. You sound like you're from back east or something."

"You got that right, shorty. New York, born and raised. What's your name?" he asked.

"I'm Lyric."

"I'm Trenton. Can we get away from this loud music? I need to be able to hear every word you say." He was totally feeling her. He led her by the hand to the foyer of the hotel and didn't stop talking until the party was over.

After that night, they were together every weekend. Her mother adored him. The more time passed, the closer they became. One night he asked her to come and see him. Rose petals led the way through his house to a hot tub out back.

Trenton knew Lyric was a virgin. She wasn't trying to give it up that night either.

"Here's a bathing suit. Just come relax with me. No funny business, I swear."

She decided it was harmless. The water was divine. Trenton knew how to treat a girl. He pulled her close to him. They began to kiss. Everything was moving so fast. Before she knew it, the bathing suit was gone. She tried to protest. But then he told her that he loved her.

She made her peace with her lost virginity on the ride home. After all, they were in love. What was the worst thing that could happen?

What was the worst thing that could happen? Those words echoed in her head as she stared blankly at her doctor, who had just confirmed her greatest fear. Pregnant! That was the only word she heard. The only good news was that Trenton was the daddy. She couldn't have chosen a better guy.

CHAPTER 4

PATHWAYS

They sat in the front office of Pathways. It was a haven for pregnant girls. Kaelynn, Yessenia, and Lyric were out of their element. It was a new environment. Their parents had enrolled them and left. They were there for orientation.

The three girls watched as other pregnant girls came in and out of the front office. Most were clearly knocked up. A few had a slight pooch that made you wonder if they were even pregnant. Some looked as though they would pop any minute. The longer they sat, the more their minds fixated on their own situation. They were here now. This was their reality.

"Girls, I'm ready for you," said the nice lady with the shoulder-length brown hair. She was pretty. Her face was kind. Her smile, welcoming. She ushered them to a conference room. "Okay, ladies, find a comfortable seat. Let's get to work. Introductions first. I'm Mrs. Georgopoulus." The girls grimaced. "Don't worry, you don't have to call me that. Mrs. G will suffice," she said. "You will be spending a lot of time together because of the way classes are structured. You three are in the first trimester, so you will be together all day. There may be other girls who enroll, but as of right now, you are it. You can start by introducing yourselves."

"I'll go first. I'm Kaelynn. I'm in the eleventh grade this year."

"I'm Lyric. I'm also in the eleventh grade."

"I've seen you around," Kaelynn said. "You go to Adams too."

"Yeah," Lyric said. She was a popular girl. Most people knew her, but she didn't know them.

"Do you want to introduce yourself?" Mrs. G asked Yessenia.

"Yeah, I guess. I'm Yessenia. But you can call me Yessie. I'm sick all the time, so forgive me if I'm not so happy to be here."

"It's okay, Yessie. We understand," Mrs. G said. "When I had my son a couple of years ago, I was sick more than I was well. Your doctor should be able to prescribe something that will make your pregnancy a little more bearable."

"Really?" Yessenia asked, puzzled.

"Yes, baby. You've come to the right place. We help guide you through school, but we also help you through your pregnancy. Now, girls, I'm not saying this is going to be easy. By no means is motherhood easy, but I'll do my best to help you." Mrs. G sounded like she meant it. It seemed like she had helped many girls before. Her calm spirit and gentle nature put them at ease. "Let's take a walk. I'll show you around," she said.

It was a small campus. There were probably twenty to twenty-five girls enrolled from all over the county. "Our numbers are lower right now. Looks like teen pregnancy is becoming less of a fad. At one point many of the pregnancies here were planned."

"I can guarantee you that this was not planned," Yessenia said.

"Mine either," Lyric said.

"Definitely not mine," Kaelynn said.

"Okay, here we are. Your new school away from school for the next eight months or so," Mrs. G said as they walked into a neatly decorated classroom.

"Hold on. We are in this one room all day?" Kaelynn asked. "I like to move around, Mrs. G."

"Well, you'll probably have a change of heart during the next two trimesters," Mrs. G said. "Your body is about to change a lot. You have to be ready for that. You will have different classes, but your teachers will be the ones moving around. This will help you later. Trust me."

"I'm fine staying still," Yessenia said. "Every time I

walk, I want to throw up." She thought about making it through this pregnancy without her "medicine." Weed seemed to be the only thing to help her queasy stomach. She couldn't wait to get home.

"Well, today is your first day. We are going to ease you into this process. It's almost time for lunch. Let's go over to the cafeteria so we can be first in line."

They could smell the lasagna before they arrived. This wasn't average cafeteria food. It looked like some love had been put into it. The ingredients were fresh. The girls could taste the difference. There was soup, a small salad bar, and garlic bread.

"This looks good," Kaelynn said.

"Not to me," Yessenia grumbled, running to the restroom. The smell of food made her sick. When she returned from the restroom, the other classes had already joined them. She opted for a bowl of soup and took a couple pieces of fruit to eat later. Then she sat with Lyric and Kaelynn.

"You okay?" Lyric asked.

"I guess. I hate this pregnancy thing. I can't believe the two of you aren't sick."

"I'm just tired," Lyric said. "I could sleep standing up."

"I threw up after I found out I was pregnant. I've been fine ever since. I have no symptoms," Kaelynn said.

"You're so lucky," Yessenia said. "You have no idea."

She sipped some soup. It was helping, but not enough. She could still feel the tinge of queasiness.

"Hey, if you need anything, I got you. Don't get up again," Kaelynn said.

"Thanks, Kaelynn." Yessenia could tell this girl was cool. She still hadn't logged her feelings about Lyric yet. She seemed stuck up. Yessenia wasn't into that. Under different circumstances, their paths would have never crossed. She was going to put up with her. But if she got out of line, she knew how to get her back in line. That was for sure.

CHAPTER 5

OH, BABY

They had been at this for a little over a week. Not much was different from regular school. Everything felt doable. They just had to keep their noses in their books and handle their business.

After lunch, Mrs. G had three boxes sitting on top of the table where she held the parenting class. She cradled a lifelike doll in her arms. If the girls didn't know better, they would have thought it was a real baby. As soon as they took their seats, the doll began to cry. Mrs. G tried to soothe the crying doll. She rocked it. Tried to feed it. And began to change the doll's diaper. When she was done, the doll made a happy noise and calmed down.

The scene shocked Kaelynn, Lyric, and Yessenia. It was all over their faccs. *This is what I am about to be faced with,* each girl thought.

"And that's how it's done," Mrs. G said when the room was quiet again.

"I can do that," Lyric said, snapping out of her shock. "I've had to do that when I was babysitting. I just can't believe it's going to be *my* life. It's different when parents slip some money in your hand and you go on your way, you know?"

"I have never been around kids. How am I going to know what to do when my baby starts crying? I have no idea what to do with a baby," Kaelynn said.

"At this age," Mrs. G started, "you are going to need a good support system. I was twenty years old when I had my first baby. I knew nothing about babies. Trust me, you will catch on fast. That's another reason why we are doing this assignment. There is a box on the table for each of you. Open it up."

They opened the boxes. Each had their own doll-baby. Mrs. G began giving them instructions. Somewhere in the process, Yessenia got up and ran to the restroom. She vomited uncontrollably for five minutes. Mrs. G knocked on the restroom door.

"I need a minute," Yessenia gasped.

"Are you okay? I brought you a toothbrush and some ginger ale. It will help."

Yessenia didn't want her help. She didn't want that stupid little doll-baby either. No way was she taking that thing home. She'd already planned on giving her baby to Dante's mom when she had it. The last thing she wanted was to be playing house. The thought made her sick to her stomach. She started to throw up again. After five more minutes passed, she left the restroom.

Kaelynn and Lyric weren't sick. The vomiting was a whole new world for them. They stared at Yessenia.

"I need to go home, Mrs. G. I'm so weak. I think I soiled my clothes. I'm just so uncomfortable."

"I understand, Yessie. Use the phone and call your mom."

"My mom is working today. Can Dante come and get me?" she asked.

"That should be fine for today, considering the circumstances. You still have to take your baby home tonight, though," Mrs. G said. "I need tonight's data to be logged."

"But I'm sick," Yessenia whined.

"I know, dear." She turned to the other two girls. "Just because you're sick doesn't mean you can shirk your responsibilities. You will be sick many days, but your baby's needs will come first."

"I'm not doing it," Yessenia said.

"But, Yessenia," Mrs. G said. "There will be plenty of days when you are not one hundred percent. But you still have to care for your child. While you wait for Dante, I'll explain the requirements."

Yessenia called Dante and joined the other girls at the table. There was nothing Mrs. G could say to make her take this doll. Absolutely nothing.

"Now, I will be checking the data. You may have a baby that has colic. A wet diaper. Or is just unhappy in its new surroundings. You are going to have to assess the baby's needs and modify accordingly."

"What's colic?" Lyric asked, puzzled.

"Colic is basically gas that comes on during the night. It can cause a lot of abdominal pain. This will make the baby cry for long periods of time. It can be very frustrating for new mothers. Your baby will respond when appropriate care has been given. That could be through cooing or burping or swinging gently. You'll have to figure it out. Your data will reveal what attempts you made to help your baby calm down. Any questions so far?" Mrs. G asked. "Also, I will be alerted to any abuse or neglect that you show these babies. Please don't make me get out of my bed because you are abusing your baby."

"It's not a baby! It's a doll!" Yessenia barked. "This is the dumbest thing I've ever heard of." She stormed out of the classroom and went to the main office. "I need to speak with Dr. Collins," she told the secretary.

Yessenia was ushered into Dr. Collins's office.

"I'm not doing Mrs. G's stupid assignment," she yelled at the program's director. Yessenia was in a terrible state.

She was weak from vomiting. She was as angry as two bulls in a rodeo. "She wants me to take a doll home and take care of it. I'm not doing that," she said defiantly.

"Well, that was actually my idea, Yessenia. I thought it would be less of a shock if you had some experience with a baby first," Dr. Collins said.

Yessenia realized she had come to the wrong place for support. "It was your idea?"

"Yes. Where is your pass? Mrs. G said you stormed out of class. What's really going on here, Yessenia? I can't imagine this reaction is over a doll."

Yessenia began to cry. "I'm *not* keeping this baby," she admitted. "I'm giving it to my boyfriend's mother to raise. I'm not keeping this baby."

"Okay, but what if you change your mind?"

"I won't."

"You might."

"I won't."

"Will you do something for me?" Dr. Collins asked. Yessenia nodded. "Just take the doll home. Get your grade so you can stay in the program. I would hate to have to kick you out over something like this."

Yessenia knew a threat when she heard one. Dr. Collins had just calmly threatened her. She needed to graduate. She had to play by their rules even if she didn't want to.

"Okay, okay. I'll take it home, but don't expect an A."

She left Dr. Collins's office and went back to class. Mrs. G welcomed her like nothing had happened. Yessenia took the doll and headed to the front of the school. Dante was waiting at the curb. She got in the car.

"What is that?" he asked.

"She's our new baby. Meet Jocelyn," she said. She was quiet for a second, deep in thought. "You're helping me with this little doll-baby contraption too. I know that."

"I know, Yessie. I've been telling you, girl, I have your back. You're just not believing me."

Yessenia closed her eyes and leaned back in her seat. She needed a breather. It had all been too much. The baby, the sickness, her visit to the office. Too much. Now she was heading home, passing the cow pastures and rice fields that lined the road.

Dante turned the car into their neighborhood. One of Mr. Robinson's horses had gotten loose and was eating the grass. Yessenia never thought she'd be trapped in this little town. She wanted more. Now this baby was threatening to take away her freedom. Freedom wasn't something she was willing to give up. Not for this baby. Not for anybody.

CHAPTER 6

UNANSWERED

Lyric was worn out. She had cried herself to sleep the night before. She felt exhausted. She listened as Mrs. G stressed the importance of having a strong family dynamic. This simulated baby project was supposed to involve everyone who would take part in raising the baby. That meant Trenton. Her parents. His parents. They were supposed to share responsibilities. She couldn't bring herself to tell Mrs. G that she didn't have a father for her child.

Her mom picked her up after school. Lyric tried to stay upbeat, going on and on about her new project. She introduced her mother to the newest member of their family, Sade Johnson.

"Shouldn't the child have her father's last name?" her mother asked, confused. "How is Trenton anyway?"

"It's a doll, Mom. Slip of the tongue, I guess."

"Well, tell him to come over soon. I'm making gumbo this weekend. You two need to work on this project together. I'm not raising your baby. I didn't have anything to do with making it. You made your bed, and *you* are going to lie in it."

"I know, Mom. I know."

She didn't want to lie to her mother. She had been trying to call Trenton for days now. He'd texted a couple times, saying he would call her later. But he never did. She was tempted to drive to his house. See what was going on.

She'd already called him too many times to count. So she gave up. It seemed like she could drown in her own tears. But she kept the pain hidden. She shared it with no one. After all, she was Lyric Johnson. Who in their right mind would dump Lyric Johnson?

She tried to keep her mother out of her relationships. The last thing she wanted was to share what she was going through and have her mother dislike Trenton. She needed them to have a good relationship.

The conversation stressed Lyric out. She knew her mom would be there for her. But she'd made it quite clear she would not be the one raising her grandchild. Lyric was scared. She was scared to be left alone. No Mom. No Trenton.

No matter what, she would be okay without their help. She had to work hard to get her diploma. Get a good job.

Maybe even go to college. She just had to. She attempted to reach out to Trenton again. He had to step up his game. She was not putting up with this.

As soon as she got home, she grabbed a quick snack and went to her room. She took out her phone and called Trenton. He *had* to answer. She willed him to pick up the phone, but it was disconnected. She tried the number again. Still the same. Disconnected.

She picked up her laptop and logged in. Was he playing her for a fool? He didn't know who he was messing with. She was her mama's baby, for God's sake. She went to his Friender page, but she was blocked. His InstaChat, deleted. It was like he was trying to erase himself from existence. What exactly was she supposed to do?

She was stressed and suddenly exhausted. She turned on VH1 and jumped into bed. As soon as she began to relax, she heard Sade crying in the other room. She had almost forgotten about her assignment!

She got up and ran to grab the fake baby. Quiet her down. Nothing was working. Frustration was starting to get to her. Her mom appeared in the doorway. She shook her head and went back to bed.

"It's just me and you, little girl. Please stop crying. I'm all you have." She fed Sade. Changed her. But still Sade cried. Lyric started to burp her. Sade let out a huge burp, closed her eyes, and went to sleep. *Not so bad*, she thought.

And it only took thirty minutes. She was proud of herself. She could do this. Nobody could tell her otherwise.

The next day at school, Mrs. G wanted to check the doll data during the parenting portion of their day. She was so preoccupied by Yessenia's lack of attention to her doll-baby that she quickly complimented Lyric's efforts and moved on. Lyric sat with Kaelynn, talking about the drama these little doll-babies were causing, as Yessenia gave Mrs. G problems for the second day in a row.

FORGET ME NOT

Lunchtime was their favorite time of day, just like regular school. It was beef-tip today, and the cafeteria workers made everything. There was macaroni and cheese, salad, and fresh-squeezed lemonade. They took their lunches to Mrs. G's classroom. Kicked off their shoes. And relaxed during the break.

"This is amazing," Kaelynn said with a mouthful of food. She took a sip of the lemonade.

"It's not making me sick. I'm so happy to get some food down. The morning sickness is getting better," Yessenia said. "Mrs. G was right. My doctor gave me some meds at the last appointment. I'm not going to say it works all the time, but it's better than it was."

Lyric moved the food around on her plate. She was

actually *losing* her appetite. The whole Trenton fiasco was sending her into a mini-depression. She didn't want to share, but the girls could tell something was wrong.

"You aight, Lyric?" Kaelynn asked.

"Yeah, you know being pregnant is kind of lonely. My friends call to *check* on me. They don't ask me to hang out with them or call to talk about what happened at school. I guess I'm just starting to feel it now. Even my best friend, Stephie, is not interested in hanging out with me."

"I'm so disconnected too," Yessenia said. She was surprised. She had something in common with Lyric. "All my friends are hanging out. My boyfriend even leaves me at home to go out with our friends. I used to be right there rolling too, but not anymore. At first I was too sick to move. Now they just don't include me. I can't wait to have this baby. For reals!"

"I guess it's just part of the process," Kaelynn said, agreeing with them. "None of my friends are really checking in right now. It's like they dropped off the planet or something. If it weren't for my dude being such a homebody, I'd have no one."

"I can't *pay* Dante to stay home," Yessenia said. "He says he's just hanging out. Whatever. If I wasn't pregnant, I'd be right there by his side. We both like being in the streets."

"Girl, you're not scared of him being around other girls? I'm not that secure," Kaelynn said. "I'd be ready to box every time he walked in the house."

"Dante ain't going nowhere. I already know he ain't checking for none of the females in my crew. Those are the only girls he's really chillin' with like that. They already know not to cross me. They don't want to see the old me. For real!"

"What about your dude?" Kaelynn asked Lyric. "He still be going out and stuff?"

"Well, he's not from here, so I can't be all on him like that. Trenton is just doing him right now."

"What does that mean?"

"Kaelynn, you are all in her business." Yessenia could tell that Lyric was uncomfortable, but Kaelynn seemed to just keep pressing.

"No, I'm not. If Lyric doesn't want to answer, then she doesn't have to."

"It's okay," Lyric said, but she was lying. She wanted Kaelynn's questions to stop. If she had the answers she was looking for, then it would be different. She didn't even know how to get in touch with Trenton, much less how or with whom he was spending his time. "It just means that we have some distance between us. We can't spend as much time together as we would like. He'll be over this weekend, though. My mom's making gumbo, so we are going to hang out." It felt bad to lie, but she wasn't about to divulge all of her business. She didn't even tell her best friends everything, much less girls she just met. They were cool and all, but it just wasn't her style.

Mrs. G came back into the classroom once they were done with their lunch. She was ready to get started on their next lesson, but Kaelynn was still in question mode.

"So, Mrs. G, is it normal that our friends don't hang out with us like they used to? We are all having similar experiences."

"Look at it from their perspectives," Mrs. G said. "Many of them are just going through high school. Their worlds haven't changed much since you were part of it. Your world, on the other hand, has been rocked. They are hanging out with the people they see every day. Don't worry about it. They'll be back in your lives in no time. You may not have the exact same relationship that you used to have, but you will probably still have one."

"That's so sad," Lyric said.

"You are all about to change a lot. Your lives are going to be different. You have to prepare yourselves for that. Your friends are going to be there, but you aren't going to be able to do the things you used to do. It's okay. You will survive the change."

"And we'll have each other," Kaelynn said.

"Aw, that's sweet, Kaelynn," Mrs. G said.

A tear rolled down Lyric's face. She wanted her old life back. Before she met Trenton, everything had been perfect. It was nice to have Kaelynn and Yessenia, but it felt empty. She wanted her friends. She excused herself to go to the restroom.

As soon as she came back, Kaelynn got up and gave her a tight hug. "We are going to be okay, Lyric. You'll see." Kaelynn saw that there was more going on with Lyric's story. Something she wasn't talking about. It was okay. She'd planned to be there for her when she was ready.

CHAPTER 8

UP AND OUT

Kaelynn, get your ass in here! Get out of bed!"

Kaelynn could hear her grandmother going off. The last thing she wanted to do was get up early on a Saturday morning. She pulled the covers over her head, hoping this would make her grandmother go away. It didn't. Again, she heard her name and more cursing.

Knock! Knock!

Kaelynn dragged herself from the bed. She stomped across her bedroom. What could be so urgent? Why was she fussing and cussing this early in the morning?

"What, Grandma?" she asked sourly.

"What? How can you ask me that? Somebody took money out of my purse, and I know it was you, little girl."

Her grandmother hadn't put in her dentures yet. Her lips were flapping. The lack of teeth distorted her mouth.

Spit sprayed on Kaelynn. She took a step back. But her grandmother closed the gap between them.

"Grandma, calm down. You must have misplaced it. I didn't take anything. Will takes good care of me. I don't need your money."

"I'm not buying that. You two are over there smoking your weed and getting high."

"And you're over here smoking your weed and getting high. Maybe one of those men you have coming in and out of here took your money. You may want to check with them. Plus, I'm pregnant. I don't even smoke anymore."

"Well, that didn't stop your mama from smoking. And it damn sure ain't gonna stop you."

That was it. Kaelynn lost it. "Don't you ever compare me to that woman! Ever!"

"The apple doesn't fall far from the tree. You are just like her at this age. Running around with a man twice your age. Getting knocked up before graduation. Experimenting with all your drugs. You think just because you have that cute little face and that tight little body you're something special. These streets done seen your kind before. Just ask your mama."

Kaelynn slapped her grandmother across the face. Her words stung. She hated the old lady. Her grandmother's face turned cold. She looked at Kaelynn with disgust.

"You get out of my house right now! And never come back. You hear me? Never!" she screamed.

"That's fine by me, you old bat!"

"After all I've done for you? I took you in when nobody wanted you. Raised you. And this is the thanks I get? You'll need me before I ever need you, Kaelynn. Believe that!"

Will was at the house in fifteen minutes. Kaelynn was hysterical. She'd called him, crying loudly. He'd tried to calm her down, but nothing worked. He could barely understand her. Kaelynn came running out of the house and fell into his arms.

"I don't know what happened. She accused me of stealing her money. I didn't take anything from her."

"Of course you didn't, baby. Is that all your stuff?" he asked, smoothing the hair from her tear-stained cheeks. She nodded. "Get in the truck. Anything else you need, we'll get it later."

He climbed the rickety steps up to the wooden porch. It was in desperate need of repair. He bent down to pick up her bags. When he stood up, Kaelynn's grandmother was standing behind the screen door, a cigarette hanging from her lips. Ashes fell to the floor as she took another puff. She stared at him coldly.

"How much?" he asked.

"How much what?"

"How much money was missing from your purse?"

"Twenty dollars is what she stole from me."

Will put Kaelynn's bags down. Then he pulled a wad of cash from his pocket and grabbed a twenty-dollar bill. He balled it up and threw it at the screen door, startling the old lady. If the screen hadn't been there, it would have hit her right on the nose.

"That's what your relationship with your pregnant granddaughter is worth to you? Twenty measly dollars? She's better off without you." He picked up the bags again and walked down the steps.

"Give her time, honey! She'll burn you too," the old lady screamed.

Kaelynn leaped from the truck and ran toward the house. She didn't know what she was going to do to her grandmother. But she wanted to make her hurt like she was hurting. *How dare she say those things to Will? How dare she?* Before she got to the porch, Will grabbed her.

"Let's go home, Kaelynn. It's *not* worth it. She's not worth it," he whispered calmly.

They rode in silence to his place. Kaelynn just stared out the window, watching the streets she grew up on pass by. As soon as they turned into the busy intersection, she could see her mom standing outside the convenience store, looking for the next person who would give her money to get high. Kaelynn could spot her anywhere. She had been looking for her since she was a little girl. Wondering if she was okay. Wondering if she was coming home. She didn't wonder those things anymore. But her internal radar was able to locate her mother in a crowd.

Kaelynn turned her head. She didn't want to look at her mother today. She didn't want to see the next guy who would pay for her mother's drug habit. She just wanted to go to Will's house. It was the only place that felt safe right now.

She had been there many times, but today was different. When they arrived, she looked around, knowing she would have to change some things if she was going to live there. His little garage apartment needed a woman's touch. That would have to wait. Today, everything was perfect just as it was. She lay down on the bed, spent and tired.

"Kaelynn, get some rest," Will said. "I'll get us something to eat later."

She slept so long, it was sunset when her eyes opened again. The day felt like a bad dream. She looked around, knowing this was her new reality. She was here in her new home. With Will. She pulled the sheets to her nose and took a deep breath. They smelled like him. She was in heaven. Too bad she'd left with so much anger and hurt. But she was here. That's all that mattered.

CHAPTER 9

A WHOLE NEW WORLD

Kaelynn lived with Will for nearly a month in complete bliss. No more riding the bus. He dropped her off at school. He gave her money. She was happy. Really happy. At school she had been the optimistic one. Now she was keeping everyone afloat. She was the go-to for positivity. Will was helping her with her doll-baby project. They took care of Jacob with ease, like he was a real baby.

When she got home from school, there was a different feeling in their little garage apartment. It was still picture-perfect with all of the decorating Will had let her do. But the blinds were closed. She could smell marijuana in the air. Smoking weed was not okay. They had both promised not to partake.

"Will?" she asked, looking for him. He was on the bed, staring at the ceiling.

"I lost my job," he said. He turned over and pulled the covers to his neck. "Close the door, please. I need a minute to think."

She had never seen him like this before. He was always the strong one. Right now he looked defeated. Weak. She wanted to help him. But he obviously knew something she didn't.

"Will? We're going to be okay." She meant for it to come out like she had it all together, but instead it sounded more like a question. He didn't respond. He just lay there. She could feel his stress. She went into the other room and opened the blinds. Sunlight could make any situation better. The last thing she should do was stress out. She made a few phone calls. She had a cousin who owned a burger place. She dialed the number.

"Bubba's Burgers," she heard a girl answer.

"Hey, is Bubba there?"

"May I ask who's speaking?"

"This is Kaelynn. Sandy's daughter."

"Bubba, phone!"

"Yo, what up?"

"Hey, Bubba. It's Kaelynn. How're you?"

"Hey, Kaelynn. Long time, no hear from. What can I do for you, li'l cousin?"

"I need a job in a bad way, Bubba. I'm sixteen now. Grandma done put me out. I'm pregnant. I'll do anything. Anything you've got is fine by me."

"Hey, I have you, Kaelynn. Come by tomorrow. We'll get you trained and ready. I just had a waitress quit. At least you can get some quick money that way. But you have to hold up your end of the deal. How's Aunt Sandy doing?"

"Don't even ask, Bubba. You know my mom."

"Yeah, I see her around from time to time. So you couldn't take that old woman anymore, huh?"

"That's a long story, Bubba. We'll have time to catch up later."

She was so excited. She could help Will through this rough patch. She thought the good news would put him in better spirits. She went into the bedroom and jumped onto the bed, waking him up.

"I got a job!" she sang.

"Kaelynn, come on. Stop bouncing on the bed," he said. "I don't want you working. I'm going to get a job."

"Well, you don't have one now. I'm going to help while I can."

"No, Kaelynn. That's my final answer. You are pregnant. It's just not right."

She grabbed his face. "You helped me. Now I'm going to help you."

☙

The plan had sounded good coming out of her mouth. When she got into it, it was overwhelming. She was juggling school. Taking care of Jacob the doll. Working. And pregnant. She was exhausted after one week. How much longer could her body take this? She wasn't sure. But she couldn't tell Will.

He wasn't very helpful. He was still upset about her job. Too bad. It was tough finding a job. He'd applied all over town. Nothing. Everyone had been laid off at the same time. They were all looking for jobs. Taking a job out of town was becoming more and more of a possibility.

"I'm going to have to start commuting, Kaelynn. I heard about a few jobs at the refineries, but they are an hour away. We can't live off what you make as a waitress. I have to work. A man has to work."

She knew he was right, but she didn't want him to go. She got in the pickup to leave for work. She only had a learner's permit but was driving by herself. The owner of their apartment appeared as she was about to close the door.

"I know your mom, Sandy. I remember when she was pregnant with you. You can't be nothing but fifteen or so. What you two have goin' on ain't right. Fix it or I will," she warned.

"Excuse me. I have to get to work." Kaelynn closed the truck door.

The woman yelled at her down the driveway. "Fix it!" She shook her finger at Kaelynn in disapproval.

Can't I ever just have a normal day? she thought as she drove to work.

Will had told her not to worry about old Mrs. Sanderson. He said she was all bark and no bite. It didn't make Kaelynn feel any better, though.

Mrs. G wasn't making this transition easy either. There was a lot of schoolwork, plus the parenting class. It was too much. Kaelynn was falling asleep in class. She couldn't tell Mrs. G everything she was going through.

The last thing she needed was her school in her business. She had to keep her relationship with Will secret. It was illegal to have a relationship with a minor. He could go to jail. She'd told nobody about her move. But Mrs. G had been probing. She saw the change in Kaelynn. It was obvious.

In Kaelynn's opinion, she just needed to get through the drama. She was treading water, with weights around both ankles. If she stopped for a minute, it would be over. She would drown. There was no time for that. Her child was counting on her.

So she kept going.

CHAPTER 10

FRIENDLY COMPETITION

Yessenia didn't have too many people she could talk to about being pregnant. Lyric was so perfect all the time. She seemed to have it all together. Yessenia never really related to girls like her. She was tough. Edgy. She lived for thrills. Kaelynn was more her speed. They talked when Lyric wasn't around. Shared what they used to do before they got pregnant. She was surprised that Kaelynn was just as much a party girl as she was.

"So what drugs have you done?" Kaelynn asked.

"I've tried just about everything. I can't lie. When I lived in the Valley, I was ten. By that time, I had popped pills. Done coke. Smoked weed. I tried crack before in my weed, but I didn't like that too much."

"Thank God," Kaelynn said. "I just like smoking my weed and drinking my beer. My whole family has been addicted at some point. My mom still is. My grand-mother—that old bat—had to raise me. I never wanted to try anything stronger than weed. I'm not proving this whole town right. I'll never be hooked on drugs like Mom."

"Do you still smoke?" Yessenia asked.

"No, I'm too scared. My baby is not coming out with weed in its system. I had to stop. Why? Do you?" she asked.

"No, but I want to."

"Look, don't, okay? You can't go there," Kaelynn said.

"I know. I won't."

That had been a week ago. Kaelynn's words had stopped her in her tracks. But today was hard. She had stopped all the other drugs she'd been into. But today she needed weed. She couldn't ask Dante. He would be furious. She called up one of her old connects and met him at the park by the house. It was cold outside now. Summer was long gone. She shivered on the bench as she waited for Ghost. He pulled up in his new black Honda Civic.

"Long time, no see," he said. She could tell he was already high.

"I know, fool. What's good?" It felt good not to be the pregnant girl for a second. She felt like her old self. She was still able to hide her little bump. No way was she about to tell him she was knocked up.

"You good? Everybody been saying Yessie dropped off the map, but here you are. You and Dante still rocking it out?"

"Yeah, we good."

"That's too bad."

"Are you flirting with me, Ghost?"

"Can't blame yo boy for trying. You know we had some good times before you got with Dante."

"That's ancient history, fool. I just need a dime and I'm out." Yessenia wasn't buying his bull.

"Your money ain't good here. Let's go smoke one. I got you."

They rolled the back streets of town, smoking and hanging out. It was a beautiful evening. They had the windows halfway down. The breeze hit Yessenia's face just right.

She couldn't be seen with Ghost. Dante would flip out. But this was much better than smoking in the park and looking over her shoulder. Ghost stopped to get some burgers. That was one thing she loved about being with him when they used to kick it. He knew how to spoil a girl.

Yessenia could see the sun going down. She knew she should be heading home.

Ghost looked down at his phone. "Hey, I need to bust this lick. You coming, or you want me to drop you to the crib?"

"Boy, Dante would catch a case if you dropped me to the crib. Drop me back to the park. I'll walk."

"See, if you was mine, you damn sure wouldn't be walking nowhere."

She munched on her food during the drive back to the park. The burger reminded her of when she and Ghost used to be together. He loved going to that little spot, the Burger Joint. He knew the owner or something. A lot of times they would get their food for free. But Ghost wasn't one to ask for favors. He always tried to pay.

She finished just as they pulled into the parking lot. "Good looking out today, Ghost."

"Anytime, Yessie." He grabbed her arm. "No, really. Anytime. I've missed you, girl."

"Ghost …" She almost wanted to tell him about the baby. She was so close. But she just couldn't. She didn't want him to look at her like everybody else who knew. "Nothing. I'll call you later. Thanks again."

He pulled away and honked the horn. She started to walk home. She wished she could go to her mom's house sometimes. Living with Dante's family made her feel homeless. At least her own child would have a good family, even if it wasn't going to be her.

The night was crisp and cold. Yessenia was still a little high. High enough not to feel the nausea that still came and went.

There was a car in the driveway. She was not in the mood for company. She didn't want to sober up. She peeked into the parked car to see if she could get an idea of what she was walking into. To her surprise, there were two people in the car, making out hot and heavy. They didn't notice her.

She couldn't see who it was until the guy pulled away with a startled look on his face. It was Dante! Yessenia couldn't believe it. She took a step back. The girl turned around and looked directly at her. *Sofia!*

"Get out of the car, Dante! Damn, Sofia! You were supposed to be my girl. Get out the car!" she yelled, banging both fists on the hood.

"I ain't trying to fight you in your condition, Yessie. Come on now. It ain't gotta be like that," Sofia said.

Yessenia saw Dante coming toward her. Her fists were clenched. She was so hurt. Somebody was about to feel her pain tonight.

"Yessie, it ain't like that. We just been spending time together. It was an accident. It'll never—"

Before he could get the words out, Yessenia punched him in the mouth, sending his head flying back. She knew she had split his lip. He was lucky that was all she'd split. Then she went toward Sofia.

"You're next!"

Sofia pulled a small gun from her purse. "I told you I'm not fighting you, Yessie. You pregnant."

"So you pull a gun on me?!" She slapped her as hard as she could across the face. "Somebody should have told you I wasn't afraid of nothing or nobody, including your little toy gun. Get off my driveway."

"You ain't got no driveway, you homeless skank!" Sofia yelled as she got back into the car.

Dante was right by Yessenia's side, trying to console her. He reached out.

"Get off me, fool!" she yelled, digging her phone out of her purse. She was tempted to call Ghost. But she couldn't take any more drama and didn't want him in her business like that.

She didn't really have anybody to call, so she called Kaelynn. She didn't know if her friend was in a position to help, but she had to try. It was almost nine o'clock.

"Kaelynn, it's Yessie. I'm sorry to call so late."

"It's okay. Are you all right?"

She started crying as soon as she heard Kaelynn's voice. "No, not really. I need a place to crash tonight. Some wack stuff went down over here. I'll explain when I see you."

"Say no more. We are on our way."

She went inside, packed a bag, and waited for Kaelynn in the driveway. Dante was out there too, trying to get her to stay. He even sent his mom to try and reason with her, but she could tell that Yessenia needed her space.

"Just know we are here for you. The street is no place for a pregnant girl."

"Tell your cheating-ass son that," she spat.

"I know he was wrong. But boys will be boys. It's something we all learn sooner or later, *mi hija*. I'm here if you need me." She smoothed her hair and kissed her forehead before going back in the house.

Yessenia could see headlights. It was Kaelynn.

"Come on, Yessie. This has been hard on me too," Dante said, trying to plead with her one last time.

"Really, Dante? Hard on you? Why? Because you're not getting any right now. Boy, bye!" She threw her suitcase into the back of the pickup and hopped into the backseat.

"Thanks," she told Kaelynn when she got settled.

"This is Will. Will, this is Yessie."

"Nice to meet you," he said.

One thing was for sure: he definitely was *not* in high school. Probably not in college either. She met Kaelynn's eyes. Her secret was safe. This was deep. Kaelynn was full of surprises. This time, she had topped herself.

CHAPTER 11

OOPS, DID I SAY THAT?

The next day at school was like one big blur for Kaelynn and Yessenia. They were so out of it. They had been up until the wee hours of the morning, talking and trying to figure out Yessenia's next move. It was a hard one. Dante had been her life—her world for far too long now. He was all she knew. But cheating with Sofia? That was something she just could not tolerate.

A whole project for Mrs. G was due that day. She had gone on and on about civil rights for the social studies class. Then tied it in with an in-class persuasive essay for English. She wanted the essay now. She allowed them to work in a group. *Thank God.*

Lyric kept questioning them about why they were so tired. They weren't ready to talk. They really didn't know what to say. Lyric came from a different world. Her family went to church on Sunday. They all lived under the same roof. She could never relate to the street life they led.

Yessenia was embarrassed. Her baby's father had cheated on her with her best friend. The fewer people who knew the better.

"Y'all are so out of it today. Do you know anything about the civil rights movement?" Lyric asked.

"You mean the war?" Yessenia asked.

"The war? Yessie, stop playing," Lyric said.

Kaelynn burst out laughing. "Now, you know she's not playing."

Yessenia smacked her lips. "Look, I skip way more than I go to class. Don't trip. I have other skills."

"Well, you need to get some legal skills," Kaelynn said. "You have a whole baby on the way."

"I don't even *want* to know what you meant by that," Lyric said. "You better not be doing any illegal stuff. That doesn't even sound like you."

Yessenia had to laugh. She had shared a bit of her past with Kaelynn the night before. Shoot! Now that she knew Kaelynn was dating somebody in his mid-twenties, she felt she could trust her with some secrets.

Lyric had no idea who they really were. She just saw them at school and assumed their relationship was shallow. But that was far from the truth.

"I have to go to the soda machine," Kaelynn said. "I'm going to pass out if I don't get some caffeine."

"You are not supposed to have caffeine," Lyric said.

"Yeah, right. I'm not giving up my Dr. Pepper for anybody. Not even my little bundle of joy."

As soon as Kaelynn had gone, Lyric started to probe. "So what's really going on with you two?" she asked. "Look, if I have to sit here and do this whole project on my own, then one of you is going to have to start dishing out some tea."

"Tea?"

"Yeah, the gossip. The scoop. What really happened last night?"

Yessenia was over it. Who cared if Lyric knew what happened? "I caught Dante cheating."

"What?!"

"Girls, are you working?" Mrs. G asked.

"Yes, ma'am," Lyric said, turning her attention back to Yessenia.

"Yeah, I had to call Kaelynn to come pick me up. I had to get away from Dante."

"What are you going to do now?"

"I don't know. I crashed at Kaelynn's man's spot last night." *Shoot!* As soon as it came out, she knew she had said too much. Lyric was nosy by nature. She was not about to let that slip of the tongue pass.

"Kaelynn's dude has his own spot? I want to come and hang out too. Y'all should have called me."

"It wasn't that type of party. It was a crazy night."

She didn't want to go past that. She focused on their project, trying to change the subject. But Lyric wasn't having it.

"What did his place look like? Is he in high school with his own crib?"

"You are trippin'. It's not that serious. He has a regular garage apartment."

Kaelynn returned from the vending machine, cold Dr. Pepper in hand. "I have a little pick-me-up. I can help now. What did I miss?"

"The fact that y'all were kicking it at your man's spot last night and didn't call me." Lyric was too smart for her own good and so naive.

Kaelynn was shocked. She couldn't believe Yessenia had spilled the beans. She hadn't even kept the secret for twenty-four hours. All that ride-or-die business. She couldn't hold water.

"I ... I," Yessenia stuttered.

"Yessie! What did you tell her?"

"Why? Wasn't she supposed to tell me?"

"I didn't tell her anything. Just that we were hanging out at your man's house. That's all." Yessenia's eyes were telling Kaelynn to chill out. She didn't want her to give up more information than she had shared. "It's good."

"Um-hm. Y'all heifers keeping something from me. I don't like it, but I'm going to chill, for now anyways," Lyric said with a smirk.

They went back to writing their essay. They knew if they didn't finish the paper, their grades would suffer. Nobody left Pathways with low grades. It was unheard of.

Focus, focus, focus.

They had their essay done and emailed to Mrs. G right as the bell was ringing. It was Friday. All their schoolwork was finished. It was an awesome feeling.

"Hey, I have an idea. Let's celebrate the weekend. Hang out at my house tonight. We can chill to some movies. My mom can whip us up some snacks," Lyric said.

"That sounds cool," Kaelynn responded.

"Does it really?" Yessenia asked. It was much different from the Friday nights that she was used to.

Lyric looped her arm through Yessenia's. "Oh, my little angry one, yes, it does sound good. Now turn that frown upside down. I haven't had girl time since I got pregnant. Come on! I need a night like tonight. Please?"

"Okay, okay. But I'm not doing facials, nails, or makeup. Don't even ask."

"Really? Are you sure? Because I have some awesome apricot—"

"Look, do you want this little slumber party of yours to happen or nah?" Yessenia asked.

"We are *so* doing this," Kaelynn said. "I need some girl time too. I like snacks. And I could use a little time away from my man," she said, bumping Yessenia and rolling her eyes.

CHAPTER 12

GIRLS NIGHT IN

It was a perfect night. Just like they'd planned. Well, everyone except for Yessenia, who vowed that there would be no nails, hair, or makeup involved. She sat with cucumber mask all over her face and a towel wrapped around her deeply conditioned hair.

"You know you loved that facial scrub," Lyric said, joking.

"Be glad I can't talk to you without making this stupid thing crack," Yessenia said.

"Shhh! You are going to crack your mask," Kaelynn warned. "I can't believe you don't love this stuff. Your makeup is always on point."

Yessenia rolled her eyes, not able to move her face much to get her point across. Once they were done, they rinsed their freshly cleansed faces and finished up the skincare routine.

"Okay, I have to admit, my skin feels good!"

"I told you. Those are some of the products my mom gets when she goes to Houston. One of the bottles of lotion she likes the most costs eighty dollars. Swear! She doesn't let me touch that one."

"Oooh, I want to try some of that," Kaelynn said mischievously.

Lyric had a sly look. She pulled herself up off the floor. "Okay, that's getting harder than it was before."

"You are not *that* far along," Yessenia said.

"We are in the second trimester already."

"Barely. We are at the end of November. We just started the second trimester. I get updates through email," Yessenia said.

"Okay, y'all stay put. I'm going to see if I can sneak my mom's bottle of Caudalie."

When Lyric left, Kaelynn and Yessenia started analyzing their surroundings. There was not one picture of Lyric with Trenton anywhere in her bedroom.

"It's so crazy. She doesn't have anything in here that even almost represents Trenton."

"Maybe it was an immaculate conception," Kaelynn joked.

"Yeah, right. She's not the Virgin Mary."

Lyric was back in minutes. The little gray bottle was in her hand. "Okay, this is the good stuff. You don't need much."

They each took a small portion into their hands and rubbed the lotion into their skin. The whole process was like a facial in a bottle. Their skin glowed.

"Omigod! I love this stuff. If I had eighty dollars to spend on lotion ..."

"Lyric, you have, like, a little dream life. Two-story home. A mom and dad who dote on you. Money. Cars. Seriously, you have it all."

"Nah, I don't have it all. Nobody does. Don't let the house and cars fool you."

"What do you mean?" Yessenia said.

"Is it Trenton?" Kaelynn asked sincerely. The way Lyric's head snapped and turned toward her, she knew she'd struck a nerve.

"Why do you say that?" Lyric asked defensively.

"I don't know. I just have a feeling, I guess."

In her head, Lyric was telling Kaelynn to mind her own business. Not to jump to any conclusions. Stop judging her. But she didn't. Instead, she hung her head in shame. What was the use of pretending anymore?

"Hey, no judgment zone. You don't have to pretend that you have it all together for us."

"Especially me," Yessenia added.

"Okay, okay." Lyric took a deep breath. She had always been such a private person. Now she was supposed to open up to these two girls. She barely knew them! She hadn't even told Stephie about the issues she was having with Trenton. Everyone could think everything was just fine as far as she was concerned.

"Spit it out, Lyric," Kaelynn said. "What's going on?"

"He's vanished off the earth. I can't find him anywhere. His phone has been disconnected. I can't access his Friender page. InstaChat is closed down too. I cannot find him anywhere."

"Nobody disappears off the earth," Yessenia said. "Tell me everything you know about him. I can find anybody, anywhere."

Lyric hadn't been to his house much. When she went, it was always at night. She had no idea how to explain this to Yessenia. She knew what school he went to. When all of this happened, she started to realize how little she really did know about Trenton Thomas. She knew he was from New York. He'd moved to Texas only months before. She knew he lived in China, Texas, now with his aunt. She knew he was sixteen. The rest had never seemed important.

"Lyric, no judgment zone. I swear," Kaelynn said. "But you are too smart for this."

"He came to see me more than I went to see him. He always acted like he just loved my family."

"Okay, who are his boys?" Yessenia asked her. "Maybe we can find him through them."

"Alien. Sam-D. And Bounty."

"Dang, Lyric! They're government names."

"I don't know. Obviously, I don't know a lot about Trenton, much less his homies. They are into some type of alligator hunting competition, though. I know that."

"Cool, that's a small community. My cousin does that too." Yessenia began searching images on the computer from the last competition. "How a *New York* boy wind up hanging with alligator hunters? That doesn't even sound right."

Lyric started laughing. "I guess he sold them too. He was always saying how he was going to get them their own show or something. They believed him too. I mean, he was from New York. The boy has swag and hustle."

"You sound like you're in love."

"I am. That's the crazy part. I fell in love with the person he sold me. I don't even know if that was really him. I'm starting to doubt it. He's probably back in New York with a whole new life."

"Yeah, an alligator hunting, music loving, high schooler from New York who dropped down in Texas may be a hard sell for most. But he had you hook, line, and sinker. I wonder who he's pretending to be today." Kaelynn shook her head at the absurdity of it all.

"Wonder no more," Yessenia said, turning the computer to face Lyric. "Dude didn't even make it out of Southeast Texas. He's not in New York. He's right there in Baymont."

"Who's the girl in the picture?" Kaelynn asked.

"Well, it damn sure ain't his sister," Yessenia said.

"I can't believe it." Lyric pulled the iPad closer to her face and stared at his image. She could hear her friends talking in the background, but she wasn't paying attention. Her focus was on the tablet screen. Trenton looked happy. Hadn't she made him happy? She thought they had something special. The girl in the picture was average, not gorgeous. She definitely didn't have anything on Lyric. *What does she have that I don't?*

"Lyric." Kaelynn was rubbing her arm. "Are you okay?"

Lyric snapped out of it, wiping the tear that ran down her cheek. She shook her head. "This girl broke up my family."

"No, Trenton did that all by himself. She probably doesn't even know you exist, Ma."

He hadn't vanished at all. Lyric realized he made her vanish off the earth. No girlfriend, no baby mama, and most importantly, no baby. He was free to live. She touched her belly, knowing she was all this baby would have. She was trying to be okay with that, but it was hard.

She just couldn't believe she'd been so stupid.

CHAPTER 13

CAN'T A GIRL GET A BREAK?

Soon it would be Christmas break. Normally Mrs. G sent their simulated babies home with students for the holidays, but not this time. Their data had hit record lows. Even Lyric, who used to be very attentive to her baby, had now started to ignore its cries. There had to be some explanation as to what was going on in their lives.

She tried meeting with them one-on-one, but they weren't opening up. It was the first time at Pathways when she could not reach her students. She was frustrated. The last thing she wanted was to lose them. She knew how important getting a high school diploma was for a young girl.

Their situations were unique. They had all gotten pregnant at the beginning of the school year. That was extremely difficult. There was no summer break to ease into the process. They had to go through the whole school year pregnant. It was starting to take a toll on them. Quite frankly, their lack of enthusiasm was starting to take a toll on her too.

It was Yessenia's one-on-one that had made the greatest impression on her. "You're not even trying anymore, Yessie. Is Dante helping you at all? Do you have a support system at home?"

She stared at her blankly. "You have no idea what I'm going through. You sit there with your cute little outfits and fresh haircuts, thinking that everybody was raised like you. Just because you got pregnant young doesn't mean we have anything in common."

"I know your situation is difficult. I know living with Dante's family is a challenge."

Yessenia laughed. It wasn't a real laugh. It was more like an *if-you-only-knew* laugh. An ironic laugh. "Yeah, that's what it is, Mrs. G. I'm uncomfortable living with Dante. Whatever. Are we done?"

Mrs. G was done. She wasn't getting anywhere. After their brief conversation, she decided it was time to go by Dante's house and see what the environment was like. She didn't want to have to turn anybody in to Child Protective Services, but something was off. Yessenia was still a minor. Something about her was crying out for help. Mrs. G wanted to know what it was.

She pulled up at Dante's house, not knowing what she

would find. There was nobody outside, so she went to the door. She knew Yessenia was not going to be happy with her for showing up unannounced.

A heavyset Hispanic woman opened the door. "Bueno," she said, eyeing Mrs. G curiously.

"Hola, is Yessie here?" she asked.

"No, Yessenia doesn't stay here anymore."

Mrs. G was puzzled. *If she doesn't live here, then where does she live?* "Do you know where I can find her?"

"No se," Dante's mom said, shrugging her shoulders. "When you find her, tell her to come home. Please."

Mrs. G nodded her head and got back into her car. Yessenia was officially homeless with a baby on the way and nowhere to go. No wonder she couldn't connect. This girl was having a rough time. Yessenia was right. Mrs. G had been lucky when she got pregnant. She had a comfortable home, siblings, and parents to help her through her hard time. This was a whole other level.

She sat in her car for a minute, taking it all in. She put the key in the ignition. As soon as she turned it, a car pulled into the driveway. A handsome boy with jet black hair and a beautiful smile got out of the car. There was a girl on the passenger's side. She had long ombre hair and a flawless shape, which she showed off in a skimpy little outfit. She wasn't very pretty, but she had flair. She threw her arms around the boy's neck and kissed him on the lips. He pulled her closer and she giggled, running to the front door.

"Dante, stop! You're going to make me fall in these heels," she yelled as he playfully chased her.

It all made sense. Mrs. G pulled away, thinking of Yessenia. She had been traded in for someone with less drama, less baggage, and no baby. They actually had more in common than Yessenia knew. She just didn't know how to tell her without letting her know she'd been to Dante's house. Maybe this was one she'd have to keep to herself.

CHAPTER 14

NEW YEAR, SAME OLD STUFF

Yessenia had been staying with Kaelynn and Will. It was hard sleeping on their little couch. They made her feel like family, but she knew they'd rather be alone. She always felt like she was in the way.

Kaelynn was working a lot. Yessenia was alone with Will most evenings. She was uncomfortable with the situation. And she knew she would have to make a move soon. She had already applied for Section 8, the program that helped families get back on their feet. In their small little town, finding housing was difficult. All of the apartments accepted Section 8, but owners had to offer only a small percentage of the residences for the program. There was a waiting list. So she waited.

ॐ

When Kaelynn finally got a day off work, they went out to

buy groceries. When Mrs. Sanderson, Will's landlady, saw them going up the stairs with their bags, she stopped working in her garden and stared at them.

"What's her issue?" Yessenia asked.

"Just ignore that old nosy bat," Kaelynn whispered.

"I can hear you," Mrs. Sanderson responded. "Tell Will if there are any more young girls on my premises, he may want to find somewhere else to live. I don't know what you all have going on, but I'll call the cops. So you may want to rethink your little plan. This old nosy bat knows people in this town."

Kaelynn ran up the stairs. "Come on, Yessie." Yessenia just stood there. "Come on!"

"Am I getting you all in trouble? My being here?"

"No, she's been threatening to call the cops since I moved in. She's just blowing smoke. No big deal."

"Does Will know?"

"Yeah, but we are not tripping on her. She likes her rent money. Trust me."

Yessenia wasn't sure if Kaelynn was being smart or delusional. But now more than ever she knew it was time for her to make a new plan.

～

A whole week went by. The girls forgot about Mrs. Sanderson's threats until they got a call from Kaelynn's grandmother. She said the cops had come by and were asking all sorts of questions about where Kaelynn lived. They said they were investigating a complaint. She told them Kaelynn lived with her. The cops said Kaelynn should be there the next time they came by. They didn't want to take further action. Her grandmother told her to pack her bags and move back home before Will wound up behind bars.

When Kaelynn told Yessenia, she immediately agreed. "You have to move back home."

"You know that nosy landlady called the cops. They will be coming here next. I don't want to go back to my grandmother's."

"You may not have a choice. Would you rather see Will locked up? That's a real consequence, you know?"

Kaelynn thought long and hard. She didn't want to burden him even more, but she knew she had to.

Will had exciting news when he got home. He'd finally found a job. They needed help on the Lott's ranch. At least he was able to stay in town. And ranching was right up his alley. It had been a long time since his days as a ranch hand. But he could run the whole show, which is what they wanted.

He told the girls to get dressed so he could take them to dinner in Baymont. To celebrate. They quickly changed and headed out the door.

The phone call from her grandmother was bothering Kaelynn. But she didn't want to ruin the night with drama, so she kept it to herself.

When they got back from the buffet, there was a police car in the driveway. "Turn, turn!" Kaelynn yelled.

"Why? What?"

"The cops are at the house, and I think I know why."

She detailed everything that had gone down. Will knew it was time to make a change. He had to be the grown-up. Their future depended on it.

CHAPTER 15

ONE LOOK

Will and Kaelynn helped Yessenia do the one thing she vowed she would never do: move back in with her mother. She could feel her stepfather's eyes as they moved over her body when she brought in her stuff.

"Pregnancy looks good on you. You're growing in all the right places, *mi hija*," he said in a drunken slur.

"You're sick," she yelled, running back outside.

"Well, it looks like I'll be going back to Grandma's, and you'll be here. It was fun having you around," Kaelynn said. "Hey, don't look so sad, Yessie. It won't be *that* bad."

Kaelynn had no idea what Yessenia had been through in this house. Her stepdad was disgusting. And her mother defended him. She couldn't understand how she could love anybody who would hurt her own daughter. But that was her mother, always in denial.

She called the housing department five times every day. When her stepfather looked at her, it made her skin crawl. She had to get out of this house. She had to get away from him.

Dante showed up on her doorstep, begging her to come back with him. She was tempted. Anything was better than being here. But he'd hurt her. She couldn't let it go. Cheating was just too much. And it was with her girl. No! She was too hard for that, too strong.

She called Ghost and got him to drop off a package. There was no hiding her pregnancy now. In this little town, she was sure he already knew she was pregnant. She couldn't deal with this sober. Baby, stepfather, mother, Dante, school. Too much! Desperate times called for desperate measures.

It was also time for a doctor's visit. The appointment was the one where you found out the sex of the baby. The one with the ultrasound that everyone who wanted to be pregnant was always excited about. The doctors and nurses told her to get ready, like she was supposed to be happy. She didn't even plan on keeping the baby. But she didn't want to give it to Dante's family anymore. She had already looked into adoption. Being a mother was not something she could or was willing to do by herself. She wasn't interested in it at all.

Before she could see her doctor, she was taken to the room with the monitor and equipment used for the ultrasound. She took out her phone and started playing a game. There was always a long wait. Anything you had to do at this office required a long wait. She lay back on the table and felt a slight flutter in her stomach. This baby was annoying. Even when she tried to relax, it moved and made her have to adjust. She wished the nurse would come in and get this show on the road.

There was a light knock on the door. "You ready, darling?" The nurse had a deep Jamaican accent, definitely out of place in this part of the world. It was something Yessenia had only heard on TV.

"As ready as I'm going to be."

The nurse took out a wand attached to the machine. She spread some gel on it. Then she lifted Yessenia's shirt and moved the wand until she found the baby's heartbeat. Next she clicked on the monitor to get an image.

"Well, well, well," she said. "You're going to want to see this."

Yessenia continued to play on her phone. "Nah, I'm good."

The nurse stopped moving the wand like she had never heard of such foolishness in her life. She looked at Yessenia. "I had a baby at your age. It's one of the reasons I went into this profession. Are you planning on keeping your baby?" She searched Yessenia's face. Yessenia focused harder on her phone. She didn't care what this nurse thought of her.

"Nope," Yessenia said matter-of-factly without ever looking away from her game.

"Well, one thing I know for sure. In life, you don't want too many regrets. You probably already have a few here and there. You don't want to regret this moment. Just give your daughter one look. She sure is a cutie."

A daughter, huh? Yessenia took a deep breath and looked squarely at the pushy, overbearing Jamaican nurse in front of her. "Why do you care?"

"I don't know. I just do," she told her honestly.

Yessenia rolled her eyes and looked at the monitor. She was stuck. She studied the picture as if it were an artistic masterpiece. A smile spread on her face. Everybody else's pictures always looked like a little blob, but she could clearly make out her daughter's features. "It's so clear," she said, looking up at the nurse. "Why is it so clear?"

"It's the 3-D imaging we are using now." The nurse was trying to hide her smile, but Yessenia saw it.

"You tricked me! Look at her. She has my cheeks. She's so … beautiful. Are you sure it's a girl?" An unexpected tear ran down Yessenia's cheek.

The nurse moved the wand down. "Yes, ma'am. It's definitely a girl."

At that moment Yessenia wanted to protect her daughter. She couldn't take the chance that this kid would have the kind of life she'd had. If she gave her baby away, then who would look out for her?

She broke down in the office. She cried for her own childhood. For neglecting her responsibilities. And for wanting to give up her baby. How would she ever explain this to her daughter? She wanted this baby! What a shock. *Us against the world, little girl. Me and you. I promise.*

The nurse got some tissues for her. She moved hair out of Yessenia's face and away from the tears. "It's okay. You're going to be okay. There's a group that helps young girls like you get the assistance they need. You tell them Miss Mae sent you, you hear?"

Yessenia took the business card and studied it. "Thanks, Miss Mae," she said. She couldn't believe she'd fallen head over heels just by looking at a little face on a screen.

She protected the ultrasound pictures. Cradling them like a baby. She studied each image as she waited to be called back for her exam. Something shifted for Yessenia that day. What did it all mean? She was actually going to be a mother. Somebody needed her to be a better person.

"Yessenia!" a nurse called her name. "Will you leave a urine sample in stall A or B, please? Then you can go back. The doctor is ready for you."

CHAPTER 16

GOTCHA!

Lyric had skipped school for a week. Yessenia and Kae-lynn reached out. They even went to her house. Lyric never answered the door. Mrs. G was constantly asking about her. Nobody knew what was happening.

It was unlike her to go missing. Mrs. G didn't want to alert her mother. She had sensed that Lyric was going through drama when her grades began to slip. She'd planned to give her a little space, but the space she needed was coming to an end.

Lyric knew it too. She knew everyone would start to question her whereabouts, but she couldn't deal right now. It was either take a minute or go crazy. She chose to take a minute. She had talked her mom into allowing her to drive to school.

"I cannot ride that bus right now," she'd said. "I feel

every bump in the road, and it's killing my back. I have my license now." She was pulling out all the stops.

"Okay, okay. But you better keep your grades up and come straight home."

Her mom had trusted her. Technically she hadn't lied. Every day she took the thirty minute drive to school, passed all the feed stores, passed the acres of rice fields and corn stalks. She was not going to just any school, she was going to Trenton's school: Baymont High.

It was two days before she actually saw him, but she did. One day she saw him leave class and get on a school bus. In her mind he was missing her. His family was the problem. They were stopping them from being together. She had made up a story in her head.

The next day she spotted him again. He was *so* fine. He was leaning against a flagpole at the front of the school. He was swagged out. She could see that even from across the schoolyard. She wanted to get out of the car and walk over to him. She was trying to keep it together. Trying to be brave. *You can do this. Let him know you are still here. Let him see your growing bump.*

As soon as she had talked her nerves up, another girl beat her to it. She knew the look in his eyes. It was the same way he used to look at her. He draped his arm around her shoulder and walked her to her car. He kissed her on the lips and walked over to the passenger's side.

Lyric felt played. It was the same girl from his Friender page. She was sure of it. *So they're actually in a relationship. He's really moved on.* She was trying to make it sink in. She had cried so much. There were no more tears. She was just angry.

She showed up at Baymont High the next day. She sat there during lunch, watching him with a whole group of people. It looked as though he had created a new life, with new friends and a new relationship. He had pretty much erased her from the picture. It was like she didn't exist. Like their baby didn't exist. And that was not going to fly.

She got out of the car. It was an out-of-body experience. Like she was dreaming. She didn't know what she was about to do or say. She stood on the edge of the group. He didn't even realize she was there.

"Say, son, I'm going to get something to drink before the bell rings. Let's go, Mego," he said to the girl who was draped under his arm.

Two steps later and he was face-to-face with Lyric. It stopped him in his tracks. At first it looked like he wanted to say something. Acknowledge her in some way. But then he looked at her growing body. He seemed to turn cold.

"Excuse me," the girl said, noticing that Lyric wasn't moving. "Do you know her, Trenton?"

"Nah, I don't know that girl," he said with a cockiness Lyric had never noticed before.

His gaze was icy cold. It enraged Lyric. She slapped him across the face as hard as she could. "By the way, it's a girl." Then she spit in his face and walked back across the schoolyard to her car.

She could hear Trenton's girlfriend. "Who was that?"

"Nobody," Trenton lied.

She almost turned back. She wanted to let this dumb girl know who she was. Wasn't it obvious? But what would be the point? She knew one day he would come looking for them. Anybody who could treat the mother of his child this way didn't deserve to be a part of their lives. She would never keep him from his daughter. But she had a feeling he wouldn't be fighting to be there any time soon. She had misjudged him. She thought he was someone else. Someone worthy of her love.

She drove until she was out of the city limits. She had to put distance between them. She stopped at one of the feed stores along the stretch of highway. The smell of farm feed and hay hit her at the door. She walked across the wooden floor to the cooler. Cold water was just what she needed.

Stuffed and mounted animals were displayed around the store. A dead alligator caught her eye. It brought her mind back to Trenton and made her want to kick it.

She paid for her drink and snack. Back in the car she opened the Payday before leaving the dirt-packed driveway. As soon as she took a bite, what she'd just been through hit her. She couldn't even chew. She spit out the candy and put her car in reverse. Dust flew as she sped away from the store.

CHAPTER 17

FAMILY FIRST

Lyric's body shook. She could barely see the road through her tears. What a *fool!* She'd been played. Trenton was a jerk. How could she be so wrong about someone?

Ten minutes later she was home. She didn't want to answer any questions. She needed to be alone. But there was a pickup truck in the driveway. Lyric parked on the street and tried to sneak by. Suddenly, Kaelynn jumped out of the truck. Then Yessenia.

Lyric fell into Kaelynn's arms, sobbing. Kaelynn looked at Yessenia, happy they'd arrived when they had. Then Lyric's mother came out of the house.

"Y'all come inside. The last thing we need are these nosy neighbors in our business. Take Lyric in. I'll get something for you girls to eat." Lyric's mother looked around the neighborhood cautiously. Luckily, they were the only ones outside. Three pregnant girls breaking down on the front lawn would cause quite a scene.

Once inside, Lyric calmed down enough to tell them what happened. They all sat around the dining room table while she described everything. Where she had been. How Trenton had treated her. And their confrontation.

"It was horrible! But you wouldn't have known it if you'd seen me," she said. "I was strong up till the reality of my situation hit me."

"He didn't deserve you anyway," Yessenia said.

"He sounds like such a bastard," Kaelynn said.

Lyric agreed. "I just feel sorry for this girl and the next girl and the next girl. I swear to you, I thought he loved me. When I saw them together, he treated her exactly how he treated me. I was just one more notch on his belt. I mean … I was so stupid. I gave myself up for that pig? What a waste."

"Look how long I was with Dante and how played I got. He wound up with one of my friends! We were supposed to be together forever. At least that's what he told me. It could happen to anybody."

"Boys just suck," Lyric said.

Lyric's mother came out of the kitchen with cookies and strawberry lemonade. She put the snacks on the table. "I've been eavesdropping for a while," she said, smoothing her daughter's hair and looking down at her. "You girls are only partially right. Some boys suck, but they don't all suck. Don't get righteous. You wanted to buy into what they were selling. You must take some blame too, or you're going to keep making the same mistakes. The other option is to be bitter and not want any relationship."

"So what are you saying, Mrs. Johnson? It's like you are telling us to love again, but don't trust again. I don't get it." Yessenia was trying to be honest. She didn't have anybody at home teaching her the ways of life. She was learning on her own.

"Yessenia, you're still very young. You have time for love. I know Dante's infidelity hurt you, but one day you will find somebody who *really* loves you. When that happens, I don't want you to be so bitter that you aren't open to his love. Don't rush anything. Be young."

"I have a baby to raise, Mrs. Johnson. I don't have time to be young and carefree anymore."

"What?" Lyric looked puzzled. "I thought you were giving the baby to Dante's mom. Wasn't she going to raise it? I thought you didn't want any part of it."

Yessenia smiled and dug into her purse for the ultrasound picture. "I can't trust anybody to raise her but me," she said, handing the picture to Lyric.

"Omigod. A girl? She's beautiful, Yessie."

"I know."

"I don't know," Lyric said, sounding negative again.

"I thought Trenton was going to be here for me. Now I'm all alone."

"Honey." Her mother grabbed her chin. "Look at me. You are never alone."

"But you said you wanted no part in raising this baby, Mom. That's what you said."

"Well, my baby, I can tell you this. I didn't bring you into this world to abandon you when you need help. Mama will always be by your side. I don't care if Trenton never shows up. Dad and I have your back. You hear me? That's the last thing you have to worry about."

Kaelynn and Yessenia were so happy for Lyric. At least she had her parents, especially her mother. They knew those were words they would never hear from their parents. It was a learning experience for both of them.

"That's the kind of mother I want to be," Kaelynn said.

Mrs. Johnson's eyes filled with tears. She realized these two teen girls were in a tough spot. "Oh, baby. Y'all are going to be wonderful mothers. Just know this, I'm here for you both too. If you need advice ... anything, I can help you. Just call me. You are always welcome here."

"Thanks, Mrs. Johnson," Yessenia said sincerely.

CHAPTER 18

CAN NEVER BE TOO CAREFUL

Kaelynn and her grandmother had been living together again for a few weeks. They had not fought since Kaelynn returned. It wasn't a perfect situation, but it was peaceful. Anything was better than Will going to jail for being with a minor. Her grandmother was trying to be understanding.

Will was allowed to come over only at night. Her grandmother was adamant. No cops on her doorstep again. The couple respected her wishes. It was enough that Child Protective Services had shown up again. That alone put Kaelynn's grandmother on alert.

Kaelynn replayed the scene in her mind.

৯

Knock. Knock. Knock.

"Yes, we are here to see Kaelynn Beeman," said a lady in a gray suit. She smelled like an ashtray and strong coffee.

"I'm Kaelynn," Kaelynn said. She protectively touched her belly, like this woman had been assigned to take her baby away.

"I need to ask you a few questions if you don't mind."

"Can my grandmother be present? I'm still a minor," Kaelynn said.

"Of course, dear. That'll be fine."

Kaelynn went to get her grandmother, who had just taken a Xanax to calm her nerves. "Grandma, a lady is here from CPS," she whispered.

"CPS?" she asked, putting out her cigarette.

"Yeah, and I need your help. I can't be alone with her."

"I don't see what I can do. What help am I going to be?"

"Come on, Grandma. You're all I've got."

They walked into the living room together. The caseworker gave them a look. She wrote something down. She looked around the room. Wrote something down again. Kaelynn could tell her grandmother was nervous, which made her nervous too.

"I just have a few questions for you. Then I'll be out of your hair. I'm sure you have a lot of prep to do for the baby's arrival. In order to get assistance from the state, we need to know where we can find your baby's father."

"Cooper, that's my baby's name. Well, Cooper's father is from New York, or so he told me. It was a one-night stand. I didn't exactly get his address," Kaelynn lied.

"Oh." The caseworker frowned. "Do you know his full name?" she asked.

"I know his first name. It's Max."

"Just Max? Does that stand for anything?" she asked.

"Your guess is as good as mine," Kaelynn said. She knew she sounded trashy. But it was worth it to protect Will. She would have to play that part today.

"Do you have a crib for the baby's arrival?"

"No."

Her grandmother came to her rescue. "She will have a crib soon. Her uncle is getting one as we speak."

Kaelynn was happy her grandmother was there. She hadn't really thought about what things the baby needed. Lyric already had a baby shower and got lots of presents. Kaelynn's family just didn't get involved like that. Her grandmother had apparently thought some of this out. What a relief. *Maybe moving back wasn't such a bad idea after all.*

The caseworker asked them more questions about preparations for the baby. Then she gave them brochures and applications for government assistance programs. She promised to return to check on baby Cooper after his arrival.

"If everything is fine when I return, then that will be my last visit. We just want to make sure your baby has his needs met."

"He will. I can promise you that," Kaelynn said.

As soon as she left, Kaelynn called Will to give him the scoop. She told him not to worry. She was taking care of everything. "They are looking for somebody from New York named Max. We are okay. Can you come see me tonight?" she asked.

"You bet. And I have a surprise for you," he said.

৯

Will came over after work, freshly shaved and smelling good. He looked happy.

"Okay, what's my surprise? Tell me!" Kaelynn asked impatiently.

"Well, I didn't want to tell you because I knew you'd be worried. Baby, I can handle my own."

"Shush! Tell me my surprise." Kaelynn was bouncing up and down with excitement. There were very few people in this world that treated her like she was worth surprising.

"Okay, okay. I placed first in the bull-riding contest at the rodeo."

She punched him in the chest. Hard. She'd lost an uncle in a bull-riding contest when she was five years old. Will knew how she felt about that. She couldn't believe it.

"Ouch, Kaelynn. Come on. There was a thousand-dollar prize. I was able to use five hundred on a new apartment away from Mrs. Sanderson. And I have five hundred for you to get Cooper some things."

Kaelynn started to smile. She grabbed his face. "Ugh,

just don't do it again," she said, kissing him on the lips. Then she punched him again.

"Ouch! Would you stop that, please? I'm sore enough from the rodeo."

"I'm sorry. I just can't lose you," she said, cuddling up to him. "Are you going to help me pick out the stuff I need for Cooper? I don't know where to begin."

"I'll take you into Baymont this weekend. We'll go shopping."

"My uncle's getting the crib. So we don't have to worry about that."

"Hey, whatever you want. I'll get it. I'm going to marry you one day, Kaelynn Beeman. Just you wait and see."

CHAPTER 19

A BLESSING AND A CURSE

Yessie was locked in her room as usual. The thought of leaving the protective space and joining the rest of her family in the living room made her sick to her stomach. They sounded happy enough. Her half-siblings were her stepfather and mother's biological children. He wouldn't hurt them. At least that's what she chose to believe.

She put on her headphones. She needed to drown out the noise. Listening to the sounds of family life made her want to run. But she had nowhere to go. She noticed a missed call from her doctor's office. *What could they want now?* she wondered.

It was still early enough to reach them.

"Yes, this is Yessenia Torres. I have a message to call the doctor."

"Hold please," the receptionist said.

After what seemed like forever, a nurse got on the line. "Yes, Miss Torres. We have an unusual lab result. We need you to come in first thing in the morning."

"Is there something wrong with my baby? What's the problem?"

"No, nothing like that. Your little girl is fine. We are concerned about you. Don't worry. The doctor will speak to you in the morning."

No matter how much the nurse said not to worry, Yessenia was worried. She called Kaelynn and Lyric, but neither of them picked up. She was in this one alone. Many thoughts ran through her mind. She slept restlessly and had crazy dreams. There was always danger with every turn of the corner. She woke up in the middle of the night to use the bathroom. She was happy to be awake. She needed a break from her dreams. But as soon as she lay down, the weird dreams started again.

The next morning she took the bus across town to the doctor's office. She was not the first one there. The wait seemed like it would never end. Finally her doctor's nurse appeared in the waiting room.

"Yessenia Torres? How are you this morning?" she asked, noticing Yessenia's apprehension.

"I've had better days. I've been up all night with crazy dreams. It was brutal."

"Crazy dreams go along with pregnancy. I had them all the time when I was pregnant with my daughter."

"Really?"

"Really. Now go ahead and leave a urine sample. I'll get you in to see the doctor."

When she was done, she waited in the doctor's office. He showed up with two nurses. "Yessenia, how are you, dear?" he asked.

Yessenia was intimidated. She couldn't even respond.

The doctor went on. "Well, we have some bad news for you. At your last visit we found a significant amount of marijuana in your sample. There have always been traces, but the amount at your last visit surprised us. We had to call Child Protective Services. They will be involved in your pregnancy and delivery now. Do you understand what I'm saying to you?"

"Yes, sir."

"Would you like a parent or guardian to be here with you? This is important."

"No, sir."

"Okay. The good news is that your sample today had lower levels. CPS wants to keep it that way. You must enroll at the rehabilitation facility for expectant mothers and complete the program before you deliver. Or CPS will not allow you to bring your baby home with you," the doctor warned.

"How will I get to school?" Yessenia asked.

"A bus will take you to Pathways. Don't worry. This isn't the first time this has happened. We'll take care of you. But we have to make sure your baby is taken care of too. Is the rehab placement something you'd be willing to do?"

"Anything to keep my baby, Doctor."

"Good. Go with the nurse. She can get your paperwork started."

Yessenia was actually relieved. She was getting out of her mother's house. She had somewhere to go, a ride to school, and meals provided. She didn't want to smoke weed anyway. She just wanted her baby to be safe. Her spirit rested as the nurse explained her next steps.

Someone brought Yessenia home to gather her belongings. There was no need to tell her mother, but she stopped in the kitchen on the way out.

"Mom, I have to leave. I don't think I'll be coming back."

"Yessie, you always come back." Her mother was still harboring bad feelings about her allegations of abuse.

"Not this time, Mom. I'm having a little girl. I'll never let your husband do to her what he did to me. This time I'm gone for good."

"Get out!" her mother yelled. "Liar!"

She could still hear her mother screaming from the kitchen, but she didn't care. Her soul was at peace. What a weird feeling. Peace.

During Yessenia's stay at the rehab facility, Dante's mother showed up. She was angry. Her grandchild was going to be born in rehab? She couldn't stand the idea.

"I'm taking this baby from you. You are unfit! The judge will see to it."

She had to be escorted out by security guards. Yessenia stayed calm. She knew she had to stay that way. Too much was going on.

The next day at school, she confided in Mrs. G about everything that had been happening.

"Yessie, you've been going through this on your own?" Mrs. G grabbed her hand and squeezed it gently. "I told you I'd be here for you, didn't I?"

Mrs. G was like an angel from heaven. She helped Yessie find an attorney that worked pro bono for girls in her situation. Yessie didn't have to pay a dime. Mrs. G also helped her file paperwork for an apartment. She made sure she had enough supplies to bring her baby home comfortably.

"Mrs. G, how can I ever repay you? You've done so much for me. More than my own family," Yessenia said, fighting back tears.

"You just take care of that baby girl. You said her name is Myla. That's all you have to do. Love her hard. Put Myla first. That's how you repay me. Deal?"

"Deal," she promised.

CHAPTER 20

ONE YEAR LATER

They met at the park. It was a beautiful spring afternoon. Graduation day was close. They were seniors. They were all going to finish high school. Their babies were a year old. One thing that hadn't changed was their love for each other.

Yessenia watched as Myla played in the sandbox. She was absolutely perfect in every way. She was relieved that her drug use hadn't affected her daughter at all.

Lyric was there with London, who always looked like a doll. She wore the cutest clothes. Lyric's mom even made matching bows for her hair. She looked like a baby model.

Kaelynn's little man, Cooper, was outnumbered. But he didn't seem to mind. Soon he would have a baby brother to play with anyway.

"I'm miserable, y'all," Kaelynn said. "It is so much

harder this time since I have to take care of Cooper. I was as sick as you were, Yessie. It ended after my first trimester, though."

"Girl, how far along are you?" Yessenia asked.

Kaelynn shrugged her shoulders. "Far enough to stop being sick and to know the sex of the baby."

"You started having sex again way too early. What are you going to tell CPS this time?" Lyric asked.

"I'll be eighteen this fall and married on my birthday. I don't care what they think anymore."

"Good for you," Lyric said. "London!" she yelled, focusing her attention on her daughter, who was close to eating a handful of sand. "No!"

"Oooh, you had the mommy voice going," Yessenia said, laughing.

"So what's up with your custody case, Yessie?" Kaelynn asked.

"Dante's family just won't let it die down."

"Maybe you should let them spend some time with Myla, then they won't feel like they have to go to court."

"That sounds good, Lyric, but I don't trust them. Too much has happened. We go to court again next month. Hopefully we can put all of this behind us soon."

"What about you, Lyric? Did you ever hear from Trenton again?" Kaelynn asked.

"Nope. It sucks for London, but I can't focus on him.

I'm trying to work out my college plans. Where to go. What to major in. How to take care of London. I want to get my degree because I have a cool business idea. A baby clothing line. What do y'all think? Oh, I brought you both gifts," Lyric said, digging into her diaper bag. She pulled out the cutest outfits for the kids. "Mom sewed them up. I really need to learn how to use that darn machine."

They gushed over the clothes.

"Tell your mom thank you," Yessenia said.

"It's absolutely the most handsome little outfit. Ever," Kaelynn said, holding Cooper's clothes up. "And it has a cap to match. Too cute!"

It had been quite a year for them. They were still dealing with the drama. Their own children were much harder to care for than those simulated babies Mrs. G had given them. Their motherly instincts had kicked in somewhere along the way, and that made the transition smoother than expected.

"Do either of you talk to Mrs. G at all?" Lyric asked as they rounded up the almost toddlers.

"I do," Yessenia said. "Mainly on Friender. But she checks in on me every so often."

"I think we should send her a picture of us today. She would really like that," Lyric said.

"Don't you think she's moved on?" Kaelynn asked. "She probably has a whole new set of girls now."

"Of course she does. Girls always getting knocked up around here. But Mrs. G doesn't forget anybody. Trust me," Yessenia said, remembering how much the teacher had helped her the year before.

Lyric pulled out a selfie stick. The girls squeezed together with their babies. They sent Mrs. G a text message with their picture attached.

She replied instantly. "Next time I'm coming too!"

Nothing had been picture perfect for any of them. Teen pregnancy was not ideal. But they had made the best choices for them. Some people had it easy. They waited. Got an education. Found a good match. Yessenia, Kaelynn, and Lyric were a jumbled mess of teenage drama and nerves. But they were sorting through it together. And being the best mothers they knew how to be.

ABOUT THE AUTHOR

SHANNON FREEMAN

Born and raised in Port Arthur, Texas, Shannon Freeman is an English teacher in her hometown. As a full-time teacher, Freeman stays close to topics that are relevant to today's teenagers.

Entertaining others has always been a strong desire for the author. Living in California for nearly a decade, Freeman enjoyed working in the entertainment industry, appearing on shows like *Worst-Case Scenario*, *The Oprah Winfrey Show*, and numerous others. She also worked in radio and traveled extensively as a product specialist for the Auto Show of North America. These life experiences, plus the friendships she made along the way, have inspired her to create realistic characters that jump off the page.

Today she enjoys a life filled with family. She and her husband, Derrick, have five beautiful children: Kaymon, Kingston, Addyson, Brance, and Harbin Rose. Their days are full of family-packed events. They also regularly volunteer in their community.

Freeman's debut series, *Port City High*, is geared to high-school readers. *Summit Middle School* is the author's second series. *Expecting* is her first novel for Gravel Road.

WANT TO KEEP READING?

Turn the page for a sneak peek at another book from the Gravel Road Rural series: M.G. Higgins's *Rodeo Princess*.

ISBN: 978-1-68021-061-3

Chapter 1

Freddie tosses his head. Prances. I know he'd like to go full out. I pat his neck. "Not now, boy. Barrel drills tomorrow. I promise."

Today, it's endurance. Building his stamina. The goal is Evans Lake. Thirty miles round trip.

The wind picks up behind me. Goes right through my fleece jacket. I twist in the saddle. Dark clouds are building. Another storm? It's late April. This Montana winter is lasting forever. I squeeze my legs. Urge Freddie to a brisk walk. His hooves splatter through muddy snowmelt.

We get to Rattlesnake Hill. It borders the McNair ranch. I could go around it. But I pull Freddie to a stop. Take a moment to decide. Realize the decision was made when I came this way in the first place.

I turn his head toward the narrow cattle trail. I don't have to ask. He takes it at a trot. Zigzags to the top. He's so loyal. Such a willing accomplice. We get to the peak. He's breathing hard. So am I. But not from exertion.

Below us lies the McNair ranch. Two-story log cabin mansion. Stable bigger than our double-wide trailer. Covered riding arena. Fenced and cross-fenced pastures. About fifty quarter horses that I can see. Someone is lunging a palomino in an outdoor arena. Too far away to tell exactly who it is. Too short and thin for Mr. McNair. Probably one of his hands. Or a new trainer. They're always hiring new trainers. The ones raved about in horse magazines.

I'm about to pull Freddie around when I see movement. Under the roof of the covered arena. Horse's legs. Red boots. A smooth canter. Could be Amy McNair. Or her mom. Or one of Amy's friends. She's quickly out of sight again. I could wait for another glance. Decide against it. I'm not that desperate.

I click my tongue. Freddie scurries down the hill. We're soon back on the trail. To hell with taking it easy. I loosen the reins. Give him his head. The wind whips my face. We sprint a good ways. I slow him down. Ask myself if that glimpse of my former life was worth it. I don't feel any better for it. So, no. It wasn't.

We get to Evans Lake. The clouds are almost overhead now. Dark. Stormy. Snow in them, for sure. The temperature has dropped several more degrees. Damn. I could have sworn it was spring this morning. I should have checked the weather report. It was stupid of me not to.

I turn Freddie. Fifteen miles to home. I don't want to

push him. But I have to. I'm not dressed for snow. He willingly speeds up. He wants to get to his oat bucket as much as I want him there.

Bits of falling ice prick my face. Then thick, wet flakes. I urge Freddie to a gallop.

Halfway home and it's a full-on blizzard. Can't see more than a few feet ahead. I tug the reins. Just as I do, Freddie trips. Goes down on a knee. I barely stay in the saddle. Right away he's up again. Walking. I should stop him. Check his legs. But he's not limping. And I'm really cold. Too cold. I didn't even think to bring gloves.

I pull my hat down tight. Wrap the reins around the saddle horn. Slip my hands under my arms to keep them warm. Let Freddie use his instincts. Guide us home.

I can just make out our stable's blue roof. I'm shivering. My teeth are chattering. I slide off. Lead Freddie inside. Quickly take off his saddle and bridle. Make sure he has water and hay. I'll have to brush him later. I need to get inside. Need to get warm.

We never heat the double-wide more than sixty-five degrees to save money. But the kitchen feels blessedly warm compared to outside. I rush to my bedroom. Change out of my wet clothes. Throw on a jacket. Wrap a blanket around my shoulders. I'm still shivering. Back in the kitchen I make a pot of coffee. Sit at the table. Hunch my shoulders. Clasp the hot mug between my palms.

The house is empty. Is it possible my dad and brothers are out looking for me? No. I left early this morning. None of them was up yet. I didn't leave a note. They wouldn't have known where I was.

I look out the window. The snow has stopped. I should get back to the stable. Take care of Freddie and the other horses. But the cold has seeped deep into my bones. I feel frozen. Like I'll never move again.

The door bangs open. Dad barges in. Followed by my two older brothers. They wipe their muddy boots on the mat. Toss their coats onto the hooks near the door. They fill the kitchen.

"Where were you off to this morning?" Dad asks.

"Gave Freddie a ride," I answer.

He grabs a beer from the fridge. "Did you get stuck in that storm?"

"Yeah."

"That came out of nowhere. You okay?"

"Just cold. Where were you?" I ask.

"In town."

My brothers grab beers too. "Hey, what's for dinner?" Toby asks me.

I glance at the clock. Can't believe it's five already. "I don't know." I shrug the blanket off my shoulders. Nothing warms me up like the male members of my family. They're better than a furnace.

"Soon, okay?" Seth says. "We're going out again."

They disappear down the hall. I set my coffee cup on the table. Stare at it a second longer. Pull myself up. Search through cupboards. Find canned stew in the pantry. Heat it on the stove. Peel a few carrots. Toss a box of crackers on the counter. Dinner is fixed in ten minutes. They're done eating it ten minutes later.

Toby and Seth stride to the back door.

"You're leaving now?" I say. "What about Mom?"

They glance at each other. Shrug their shoulders. Seth says, "Tell her hi for us."

"Tell her yourself! You can't wait a few minutes?" Then I see Dad is joining them. "You too?" I say.

"We're going to the basketball game. Garth's son is playing. Saw him in town. Promised we'd go. Cheer for his kid." He runs his hand over his bald head. "Tell her ... I miss her. Okay?"

They're out the door. The kitchen is empty again. The temperature drops a few degrees.